The Great Indian Tee and Snakes & Other Stories

WINNERS OF THE COMMONWEALTH SHORT STORY PRIZE 2020

The Great Indian Tee and Snakes
& Other Stories

WINNERS OF THE COMMONWEALTH
SHORT STORY PRIZE 2020

The Great Indian Tee and Snakes & Other Stories:
Winners of the Commonwealth Short Story Prize 2020

This edition has been published in 2020
in the United Kingdom by Paper + Ink.

www.paperand.ink
Twitter: @paper_andink
Instagram: paper_and.ink
Patreon: https://www.patreon.com/paper_ink

1 2 3 4 5 6 7 8 9 10

ISBN 9781911475453

A CIP catalogue record for this book is available from the British Library.
Jacket design by James Nunn: www.jamesnunn.co.uk | @Gnunkse
Printed and bound in Poland by Book Press: www.bookpress.eu

CONTENTS

CONTENTS

ABOUT THE COMMONWEALTH SHORT STORY PRIZE

The Commonwealth Short Story Prize is administered by the Commonwealth Foundation, through its cultural initiative Commonwealth Writers. The prize is awarded for the best work of unpublished short fiction (between 2000 – 5000 words). Regional winners receive GBP 2,500, and the overall winner receives GBP 5,000. It is free to enter and open to citizens of all the countries of the Commonwealth. Entries may be submitted in Bengali, Chinese, English, French, Greek, Malay, Portuguese, Samoan, Swahili, Tamil and Turkish, as well as translated into English from any language. The international panel of judges selects one winner from each of the five Commonwealth regions (Africa, Asia, Canada and Europe, the Caribbean and the Pacific), one of whom is chosen as the overall winner.

CSSP 2020 Judging Panel

Chair: Nii Ayikwei Parkes
Africa: Mohale Mashigo
Asia: William Phuan
Canada and Europe: Heather O'Neill
Caribbean: Elizabeth Walcott-Hackshaw
Pacific: Nic Low

About Commonwealth Writers

Commonwealth Writers, the cultural initiative of the Commonwealth Foundation, helps develop, support and connect writers across the world. It believes that well-told stories can help people make sense of events, engage with others and take action to bring about change. It is committed to tackling the challenges faced by writers in different regions, and works with local and international partners to identify and deliver a wide range of cultural projects and platforms, including *adda*, an online magazine of new writing.

www.commonwealthwriters.org
www.addastories.org

About the Commonwealth Foundation

The Commonwealth Foundation is an intergovernmental organization established by Member States of the Commonwealth. Uniquely placed at the interface between government and civil society, the Foundation works to support civil society engagement in shaping the policies and decisions that affect people's lives.

THE GREAT INDIAN TEE AND SNAKES

KRITIKA PANDEY

The girl with the black *bindi* knows that she is not supposed to glance at the boy in the white skullcap, but she does. The boy moves restlessly on a stool as he cradles a cup of chai in his hands. The girl has flavoured it with cardamom at no extra cost before swallowing the leftover pod so her father won't find out. He is the moustachioed owner who cleans his ears with Q-tips at the cash counter. The girl looks up from the boiling contents of the saucepan, pretending to notice new customers while examining the contours of the boy's stubbly chin, the kite-shaped birthmark on his neck. He mostly watches the speeding vehicles on the road. Once in a while, he meets her gaze and his ears turn crimson. At such moments the girl and the boy realize that they must immediately look away, but never stop noticing each other wherever they go.

●　●　●

It is September. Hawkers appear with baskets of tomatoes. They are overpriced but surprisingly red. The girl's father asks her to buy two kilos. They would keep tomato chutney on the menu until tomatoes become wholly unaffordable in the winter. She squats at the water pump outside the stall to wash the tomatoes, facing the boy, gazing at the stubbed toe sticking out of his sandals. He is one of the few customers who prefer eating *keema samosas* to *aloo samosas*, but it is the least of the girl's concerns. Their stuffings are somewhat different, but the girl makes both types of *samosas* with the exact same batter. They are the same thing unless one absolutely wants to differentiate, which most people do – including the girl's father, who has strictly warned her against eating *keema samosas*.

A chilly breeze leaves the girl covered in goosebumps.

"Why does it have to get cold?" she says to no one in particular.

"Seasons change," says one of the men sitting next to the boy. They are daily wage labourers who ask for *aloo samosas* with their chai, not *keema samosas*, never *keema samosas*. They carry grimy shovels and miss no opportunity to talk.

"Because this is how it is."

"Because this is how it's always been."

"Because the Earth moves around the sun," says the boy.

The girl breathlessly punctures a tomato, then washes the red mush off her fingernails. She has never heard him speak before.

A man eyes the monogram on the boy's shirt. "Go to school?"

He nods yes.

The girl's father had pulled her out of school after a couple from Class 10 eloped to Mumbai.

The man chuckles. "I went to school myself. Now I shovel cement and sand."

Later that night, the girl can't stop wondering if the Earth really moves around the sun. Why had no one told her that? Who was making it move? She sits up in bed and thinks about endless fields of cauliflower and tries not to throw up, like she has to do on the Giant Wheel at the funfair. Dreams take over when she falls asleep. She grabs the boy's stubbed toe as they fly off the face of the Earth.

* * *

The town is on a plateau formed by colliding landmasses when the dinosaurs were still around. It is big enough to have a Domino's, but too small for traffic lights. The traffic policemen take breaks from signalling vehicles to rub lime and tobacco in the palms of their hands until drivers yell at them to regain control. The girl's father had moved here when growing onions in the village farmlands stopped being profitable. It was raining less and less each year. For a while he tried to find work at the department store with glass walls, and to live in a house with bedrooms.

Then he gave up. He got bamboo sticks and tarpaulin and set up the stall outside their shack. It unsettled him to include *keema samosas* on the menu, but he wanted to make whatever profit he could.

A painter demanded 500 rupees to adorn the aluminium anterior of the table where the chai was prepared on a coal stove. "It better be a nice and important name," the girl's father had told the painter, who could hardly spell, and so the tea and snacks stall was christened THE GREAT INDIAN TEE AND SNAKES.

The painter had promised: "Anyone who loves this country will love this name." Some passers-by point out the sign to each other and have a good laugh. Others nod in admiration of what they take to be high literary nonsense. Many click pictures.

● ● ●

The girl is frying *samosas*. Today the boy is being questioned by the men with grimy shovels about what brings him to this part of town every weekend.

"I water an old man's geraniums," he says.

"Gera-what?"

"Flowers."

Thanks to the labourers' interest in him, the girl can now hear the boy talk.

"*Germium*," she says to a golden *samosa* floating in oil, pleased that the boy knows such words. Her father glares at her. She sighs. If only she were allowed to talk to the boy, she wouldn't have to talk to the *samosas*.

"Pays well?" A labourer asks.

"Six hundred per month," says the boy.

"For watering flowers!"

"*Kya kismat hai.* Lucky bastard."

The boy says that his wealthy employer lives by himself and reads magazines with high-definition photographs of wild felines. When someone brings up the new prime minister's yoga moves, the boy silently nibbles on his *samosa*. The girl mumbles things that she wishes to say aloud to him.

"Plants make their own food. I know because I used to go to school as well ... I also know that we can't see air, but it's there ... Do you like summer or winter? I like summer for the mangoes. I don't like winter because the cold makes me feel more feelings ... I don't care if you eat this *samosa* or that *samosa*. Just saying. People should eat whatever they want to. Why is it a big deal? ... You have nice fingers, you know ... Every morning, some men gather in the park with Gandhi's statue and force themselves to laugh. If you look at them, they'll make you laugh too. They say it makes you happy ... You have really nice fingers ... Do you like me?"

●　●　●

The girl's father wants the boy to be served chai in stainless steel cups only. If the girl mistakenly serves him in ceramic, her father waits for the customers to leave, then smashes the cup. "Steel can be washed with soap and water," he says, "but you can't wash a *keema*-eater's saliva off of clay." The girl used to follow her father's orders and throw away the ceramic pieces. But now she collects them as if they are artefacts. When her father is snoring at night, she steps out of the house, glues back the broken cups under the streetlight and hides them among the tangled roots of a Banyan tree.

* * *

The girl believes that her father is kinder than he appears to be. He could have tossed her into the river after discovering that she was not a boy, but he did not. Not even after her mother, his wife, died a week later from excessive bleeding. The girl obviously doesn't like that he expects her to be up around five in the morning to open the stall, calling her the "Queen of England" when she sleeps in. However, he lets her spend on nail polish and newspapers, from which she cuts out pictures of the oval-faced woman with shimmery eyelids. The man at the newspaper stand says that her name is "Beyoncé". The customers at the stall eat *samosas* from scraps of newspaper with Beyoncé-shaped holes in them.

At times when the girl gets a bridal *mehndi* assignment – she is a decent henna artist – her father takes care of the stall so she can spend hours painting the hands of brides. She hides the names of their future husbands amid swirly, intricate henna patterns.

Nevertheless, as far as the *keema*-eater is concerned, the girl must not get ahead of herself. Her father doesn't need to tell her that girls with black *bindis* are not supposed to feel this way about boys in white skullcaps. She knows.

* * *

The girl wakes up with cold toes. She gathers twigs, leaves, bits of paper, cloth and empty Lipton cartons before setting them on fire. Her father fans the flames. The girl, the boy, four of the labourers and the girl's father sit around the fire with their chai, yawning. Sunrays are trapped in fog. The morning feels like evening. The unbroken-broken cups hidden among the Banyan's roots must be covered in frost, the girl thinks, wondering if she should show them to the boy. But what if he has a girlfriend at school? What if he has held her hand? When a labourer coughs, the boy says that his mother coughs all the time. Something is wrong with her lungs.

"I'll become a doctor and treat her," he adds.

"Treat us also," jokes the labourer.

The boy smiles. "I will."

The chai has finally awakened the men. They won't stop talking now.

"People should be able to become whoever they want to be."

"But the problem is that there are too many people."

"And too few things one can become."

"And fewer things one can sell to buy rice."

Their laughter is followed by silence.

"I want to become Beyoncé," the girl says.

"Who?"

* * *

The new prime minister's face is everywhere. On telephone poles and park benches and garbage cans and the backs of cars and even on the faces of so many people who wear masks of his own face with tiny holes for eyes. The girl doesn't know how his face appeared on the water pump outside the stall. Sometimes she is unable to flavour the boy's chai with cardamom for fear of the prime minister watching her. Other times, she skips the cardamom because, for all she knows, the boy doesn't even care.

●　　●　　●

THE GREAT INDIAN TEE AND SNAKES is out of sugar. The girl walks to the grocery store. Tiny rocks push into the soles of her feet through the cracks in her *chappals*. Once she had stolen a pair of cat-printed *chappals* from outside the temple, but they have been lying under her bed ever since. She worries that the owner might spot them and take them away.

The grocer is an old man who is partially deaf. The TV in the store needs to be pounded from time to time to keep the images from splintering. The place is packed during the cricket season, when people stop by to watch an over or two and praise or curse Dhoni. After purchasing the sugar, the girl is too caught up watching, on TV, the magnified inside of somebody's mouth being cleansed by a toothpaste that tastes like turmeric to notice when the boy appears next to her. He asks the man for chewing gum.

"Hey," he says to the girl.

"Oh, hi."

The boy is standing right next to her in a place where her father's gaze is not upon them. She can touch the kite-shaped birthmark on that neck if she wants to. The man has left a pack of gum on the counter before returning his attention to the TV.

"Nice to see you outside the stall, for a change," the boy says.

"Same."

"You'll make a good Beyoncé. Probably better than Beyoncé herself."

The girl touches her *bindi*, smiling, telling herself that she was wrong about the boy having a girlfriend at school. "Won't you offer me chewing gum?"

"Absolutely."

The girl chews the gum until it's time to go to bed; then she swallows it.

● ● ●

The girl examines ordinary objects with newfound fascination – a matchbox, a potato, freight trucks on the road, the ground beneath her feet – thinking that nothing is bigger or smaller than it should be. Everything is the perfect size. She air-dries her shampooed hair in the afternoon sun instead of twisting it up in a towel. She wonders if this is how girls become women. One night, when she is putting back together a broken cup soiled with the *keema*-eater's saliva, blood gushes out of her finger like water from the pump. Nevertheless, unlike the brides whose hands she paints with henna, she feels no need for a husband and a house and a washing machine and a baby and a mixer grinder to be content. All she needs is for the boy in the white skullcap to drink chai and eat *samosas* at the stall so she can watch him watch her.

● ● ●

The labourers are talking about an upcoming cinema hall in town that will play three movies at once. The boy is eating a *keema samosa*, waiting for his chai. Around a dozen young men with saffron bandanas arrive on motorbikes. They order chai and *aloo samosas*. The girl's father tells them to leave, because they never pay. "This isn't a wedding you can crash anytime," he says.

"Don't be so touchy now," says a young man. His T-shirt is just as saffron as his bandana. He looks like a carrot.

"Extra spicy *samosas*, please," another young man tells the girl.

When the girl's father stands up to protest, the young man who looks like a carrot pushes him into his chair before noticing that his companions are still struggling to park their motorbikes. "Who the fuck left this bicycle here?" he hollers.

"It's mine," says the boy in the white skullcap. He starts moving his bicycle, but the young man stops him.

"You think this is the fucking Olympics?"

"I am sorry. I'll move it."

"'Sorry' won't do. Say, 'chai is great'."

"*Haan?*"

"Say it."

"Chai ... chai is ..."

"You don't like chai?"

"I drink it every day."

"So say it! "Chai is great!""

"Chai is ... great."

The girl whips the batter slowly. She would poison the *samosas* if she could.

"Good. Now pick up your disgusting *samosa* and throw it away."

"What?"

"You deaf?"

"No more *keema samosas* for you," says another young man. "Only *aloo samosas* from now."

"But I like *keema samosas*," says the boy.

The young man who looks like a carrot slaps him. The girl stops whipping the batter.

"Throw your *samosa* away or we'll boil you with the chai."

The boy does as he is told.

The young man takes off his saffron bandana before handing it over to the boy. "Now get rid of that dumb skullcap and put this on."

"I won't."

"You won't?"

This time the boy looks into the young man's eyes. "I will not do that."

The young men beat up the boy, calling him a "fucking *keema*-eater", telling him to go back to his *keema*-country. One of them makes a video on his phone. The girl's father and some of the labourers try to intervene unsuccessfully.

The girl begs the men to let the boy go. "All he does is water flowers!" she screams. Nobody listens. A couple of labourers join in after some time, calling the boy names, thrusting their shovels into his stomach.

"But he is going to become a doctor and treat you!" The girl pleads. "How could you forget?" Her father yells at her to go into the house. The boy looks like a punctured tomato and dies.

●　●　●

December is almost over. The girl with the black *bindi* weeps when she is cold. She cannot stand straight. She cannot hold her head high. She cannot feel her nose. When her father wakes her up in the mornings, she turns her back towards him. "No," she says. She sneaks out *keema samosas* from the stall before eating them hidden behind the kangaroo-shaped trashcans at the park. She has never eaten anything with *keema* before. It tastes like tears until she realizes that she needs to stop crying while eating. After that, it tastes like food. Newspapers carry front-page pictures of the boy in the white skullcap, sitting against a plain grey background in even lighting, unsmiling but alive. He looks straight at her. Now, instead of Beyoncé's pictures, the girl cuts out every picture of the boy from every paper before burying them under her mattress. She wipes the frost off the unbroken-broken cups under the Banyan tree.

●　●　●

When the wedding season arrives, the girl has too many henna assignments and not enough time to grieve. The brides talk while getting their hands painted because the girl listens. One of the brides points to a picture on the wall. Her fiancé is holding the Taj Mahal in the palm of his hands. Another bride tells the girl that her fiancé's name is Adithya-with-an-H. She wants his name on both her hands, front, and back. Another asks her to feed her chocolate after her hands are covered in *mehndi*. Yet another suggests the girl play hard-to-get if she ever wants her boyfriend to propose for marriage. "Love requires you to be something of an asshole," she says. And yet another woman looks uninterested in all such matters despite her Banarasi *saree* and eye makeup, despite the jasmine flowers in her hair, as she spreads her hands before the girl. She doesn't even remember her fiancé's name. The girl tells her that it doesn't seem like she wants to get married.

"I don't."

"What do you want to do, then?"

"Paint pictures of the sky."

"You can do that even if you're married."

"I can do that even if I'm not."

"But why the sky?"

"Because it is infinite."

●   ●   ●

Newspapers are covered in pictures of a high-speed train by the time the weddings are over. There's a nationwide ban on *keema samosas*, *keema naan*, *keema parathas*, *keema pakoras* and, basically, *keema*-everything. The girl loiters in the park with Gandhi's statue.

In the mornings, the group of men stand in a circle and force themselves to laugh. They are loud and self-assured, the type that eat *aloo samosas*. At first, they go, *"Ho-ho, ha-ha, ho-ho, ha-ha."* Before long, however, they are laughing uproariously, teeth bared, arms raised in the air. The girl wonders if they had seen the front-page pictures of the boy in the white skullcap. In the evening, young men and women take too many selfies against the fountain. The young women wear lipstick; the young men have their hair sticking up. Their faces change when they point their phone cameras toward themselves. The girl wonders if they have ever tasted a *keema samosa*.

Men in blue uniforms water the plants in the park. One of them is watering a bed of flowers. The petals are purpler on the inside than the outside. She walks up to him.

"Sir, are these germiums?"

"What are you talking about?"

"Are these germium flowers?"

"There are no flowers by that name."

She walks up to another man who is watering potted yellow flowers with long, spaced-out petals, and repeats the question.

"No," he says, "but nice tits."

●　　●　　●

The girl sits on a park bench and tries to fall in love again. She tries to fall in love with the boy in an oversized T-shirt who is kicking a football, or the one who is doing push-ups, or the young man with the shocking blue earphones, walking with his hands in his pockets, or the boy who is holding hands with a girl who has streaks of red hair, or the one lying on his stomach, reading a book, or maybe even the one who is ogling at the women practising yoga. Nothing happens.

Then she lies on her back and stares at the infinite sky. She hopes the woman who didn't remember her fiancé's name is painting as many pictures of the sky as she wants to. But infinity is not the girl's type. She needs something more measurable than that, something smaller than the sky but bigger than a *samosa*.

●　●　●

It is a pleasant April morning. The men who force themselves to laugh are laughing like there's no tomorrow. One of them notices the girl sitting by herself and invites her to join them. "Guaranteed to make you happy," he says. She reluctantly accepts. In the beginning, she stands there, wanting to disappear. Then, encouraged by the men, she smiles a small, confused smile. Then she laughs softly because everyone else is laughing. For a few minutes, it feels insincere, but after that, she is actually laughing aloud. She bookmarks this as an important skill.

A man turns to her when it's over. "So, young lady, are you happy now?"

She looks at the beads of sweat on his forehead, laughter lines around his mouth.

"Are you?" she asks.

WHEN A WOMAN RENOUNCES MOTHERHOOD

INNOCENT CHIZARAM ILO

Read this between clenched teeth, a taut smirk plastered on your face. Try to taste each word as if it will escape from your mouth, like air.

When a woman renounces motherhood, no one asks her why she did it. How dare you give up on such a beautiful thing; nature's call embedded in your vagina, crested on your breasts?

Read this as if you're running out of breath. This is the same pitch your mother uses to greet your father's friends who walk past her kitchen as she alternates between fanning the charcoal stove and plucking the chicken.

When a woman renounces motherhood, she

is forced to walk from her house to the stream, a clay pot filled with ash balanced on her head, and tell the whole world how she has failed as a woman.

Read this in the many voices of women who tattle about "My husband this" and "My husband that" in hair salons.

When a woman renounces motherhood, we will point at her and say to our daughters: "This is what a woman should never become."

Read this in the cacophonous chatter ndi umunna *use to decide the fate of women.*

When a woman renounces motherhood, we must cuddle and pet her husband. His *chi* must be stonehearted to have left him in the hands of such a woman. One of us will volunteer to find him a new wife – that is, if he has not already found one for himself.

Read this and try not to feel anything.

When a woman renounces motherhood, she leaves what used to be her home with nothing. No money. No children. No anything. And God help her if she does this in old age, when she can longer fend for herself.

* * *

The telephone ringing in the parlour jars with the tranquillity of the afternoon.

"Caro," Nwakaego calls from the bedroom. The telephone pauses, as if to catch its breath, and then continues to ring. "Caro!"

Still no response. Caro, Nwakaego's housekeeper, must have left the house without telling her again. She probably forgot to lock the back door as well, the same way she did the last time … and the time before that. Nwakaego makes a mental note to resound it in Caro's ears when she comes back, that sneaking out so she and Kunle, Mrs Kasandra's live-in driver, can fondle themselves in the backyard is not more important than the security of the house. Every day, news of Area Boys wandering into homes with unlocked doors in Lagos floods her social media feeds. Everybody talks about it; in church, at work, in the mall down the street. Last week, they burgled her friend Anaeto, who had forgotten to lock her door when she got back from work. "I was in the shower when they came in. Thank God they did not check the bathroom. If not, we'll be telling another story," Anaeto said to Nwakaego when she visited her the morning after the robbery.

Nwakaego shoves aside the pile of paperwork she was working on before she slept on the bed and heads to the parlour for the telephone.

"Nwakaego, *kedu*? How are you?" Her mother's voice rasps through the tiny holes of the receiver.

"I am fine, Mama. I hope all is well?"

"*Nne*, all is not well. I have decided to renounce motherhood. *Kpa*, I am not doing again."

Nwakaego's palm tightens around the telephone, as if it will squeeze out what she has just heard. "Why now, Mama? You've been a mother for thirty years!"

The woman at the other end of the line clears her throat. "*Nne*, it's long overdue. Your father has always found a way to make me stay, reminding me of how Emeka, you and the twins need me, and the consequences that will come from me leaving. Not this time."

"When is the renouncement?"

"The day after tomorrow."

"That soon?"

"Yes. I want to do it quick-quick. I don't want any of you to make me see reasons not to do it. Let me hang up and call the twins. I've already spoken to your elder brother, Emeka."

"Mama, lemme call someone. I have a friend who works with Amnesty International. You shouldn't do this, it's fucking 2019."

"*Ibiakwa*, you have come with your abroad talk," Nwakaego's mother chuckles. "When Barrister Obiageli renounced motherhood last year, she brought policemen to protect her from *you know. Iya sikwa*, they said none of the policemen could move a limb until the ceremony was over."

"That's superstition, *biko*."

"*Nne*, save your breath."

"I'm coming back tomorrow."

"*K'odi*. We'll see tomorrow."

Long after the telephone let out a dying beep, Nwakaego continues to wonder what has gotten into her mother's head to make her decide to renounce motherhood. All these years, her mother has nurtured four children and a husband, blown coals to make fire even though it reddened and stung her eyes all night, scrubbed oil stains off her husband's singlets and helped the children find their missing socks on school days. She never complained or paused to think of herself: what she wanted, the things she needed from her children or her husband in return. A wry smile was always plastered on her face, even on Saturdays when she sat under the udala tree and stitched up the parts of her skin that had torn under the weight of being a mother.

The back door creaks, disrupting Nwakaego's thoughts. She senses it must be Caro sneaking back into the house. Nwakaego walks into the kitchen, just in time to find her housekeeper gently letting go of the doorknob.

"Good afternoon, Madam. I go outside make check if the cloth wey I wash for afternoon don dry." Caro reels off her rehearsed explanation before Nwakaego can even open her mouth.

"Shebi you and Kunle don dey do una suwegbe for backyard? Issorait. Continue." Nwakaego loves her newfound pidgin English-speaking prowess, even though her friends have told her how horrible it sounds with an Americanaccent infusion. Anaeto nearly laughed her neck off when Nwakaego said *juarè* instead of the conventional *jare* at another friend's wedding, the week before.

"Madam, I swear na cloth I go check. They never dry. One of them fall for ground sef, I come rewash am. If you think say I dey lie go ask ..."

Nwakaego waves at Caro to stop talking and rustles up a stern look. "Lock my door before going to see your boyfriend."

"I no get boyfriend. True to the Most High Everlasting God." Caro rubs dust off the kitchen floor with her right index finger, licks the tip and points towards the ceiling.

"Na you sabi," says Nwakaego. At this point, she is tempted to give Caro *the talk*. You know, basic sex ed, how whatever she is doing with Kunle – no matter how harmless it seems – can result in something else. But she decides against it. Anaeto nearly got herself into big trouble when she gave her housekeeper a pack of condoms. The girl had called her mother in the village and told her that her Madam in Lagos wanted to turn her into a prostitute. Nwakaego will give

Caro *the talk* eventually, but not today, when her mind is running haywire with her mother's call.

"Wetin Madam go chop this night?"

"Plain coffee. No milk. No sugar."

"Na so so coffee and tea una dey chop for Hafad."

"It's 'Harvard'."

"All na the same."

Caro and Nwakaego break into synced laughter. It is almost impossible to get angry with someone like Caro.

Later in the evening, as she sits on the bed, sipping coffee and folding the clothes for her journey the next day, Nwakaego remembers how her mother will often remind her that motherhood is a vocation, something that one gives one's all to without expecting anything in return. A sacred cross. A burden one cannot put down. If any woman will renounce motherhood, it certainly should not be her mother.

● ● ●

"Onitsha! Onitsha! 'E remain one make 'im full,"

a tout yells and bangs his fist on the bumper of a rickety Peugeot 504. Crumpled *naira* notes rear their edges through the fold of his right palm, as if struggling for fresh air. He wipes his brow from time to time with a torn Arsenal jersey strapped across his chest.

"One chance. Madam, you dey go?" The tout asks Nwakaego. She shakes her head and drags her box to the other side of the park. She is indeed going to Onitsha, but certainly not in an unregistered *akanelu* that might stop halfway to her destination. "All these *oloshos* wey full Lagos." The tout makes to spit, but the spittle sticks to his jaw. "You go talk say you no get money to travel."

His voice rings clear. Everybody in the park stares at Nwakaego. Some nod in affirmation with the tout while the others shake their heads in pity and give her reassuring glances.

"She be responsible woman," another tout says.

"See her short skirt. *Na olosho joor.*"

"But she no wear yellow eye shadow."

After close to an hour of scouring the park,

sifting through cars and making judgments about drivers and conductors, Nwakaego finally boards a bus. Between the man who is sitting beside her, using every gallop pass to *mistakenly* touch her breasts, and the evangelist screaming about repentance and hellfire, Nwakaego wills herself to prepare for what lies ahead. She had tried to reach the Onitsha Divisional Police Command on phone the night before, but could not get through. When she finally contacted them earlier this morning, they told her that *the Nigerian police do not meddle in native customs and tradition.*

"*Oga*, stop touching my breasts!" Nwakaego bursts out as the bus plunges into another pothole. The man sitting beside her adjusts his spectacles and mumbles an apology.

"Madam, calm down. Na just breast the man touch, he no off your pant," the man sitting directly behind Nwakaego says.

"Why should I calm down?" Nwakaego shoots back.

The evangelist seizes the moment to continue her preaching: "Brethren, praise the Lord. Can we now see how Satan manifests to thwart the gospel of Jehovah."

●　　●　　●

"Mama, good afternoon."

"Nwakaego, *ibata* go. You are back."

Her mother's response is forlorn. She does not even stand up to hug Nwakaego and say *nnua* or ask how Lagos's heat has dealt with her *one-an'-only* daughter. Nwakaego lodges her box against the wall, but still her mother does not look up. Her hands are busy with the loom at the other end of the room, between the bags of *egusi* and the *akpati* filled with her old *lappahs*.

Kpa. Kpa. The loom's wooden frame bounces away.

"Mama, *ke k'ime*? How are you?" Nwakaego goes over to the loom and hugs her mother's shoulder. It is supple now, the shoulder. The last time she visited, her mother was so bony she had to buy an extra tin of Ovaltine and Peak Milk.

"I have never felt this good in a long time," Nwakaego's mother says. She snips a knotted thread with a pair of scissors, straightens the fabric so as not to tangle the warps with the wefts and stops weaving. Her face glows when she looks up at her daughter; the seemingly permanent wrinkles and blemishes are all gone.

"I am weaving the *lappah* I will wear tomorrow in front of *ndi umunna* and tell the whole world I am done being a mother." Apart from the frayed edges of the *lappah*, the weaving is almost done. Wavy red and blue lines run across its warm, black background. "See, it is soft-soft, like wool," Nwakaego's mother says as she pushes the *lappah* against her daughter's chin. "I went round and round Nkpologwu market before I could find the perfect thread for this weaving."

"What happened, Mama? Why are you renouncing it now?"

"Go and ask that pig."

"He is not a pig, Mama. He is still my father." Nwakaego pulls up a low stool from under the loom and sits down.

"Support him like you always do."

"I am not supporting anybody."

"For thirty years, I have soaked my palms in

boiling water for that *yeye* man. I have never asked for any payment or reward or even a spiteful 'thank you'. I can tolerate your father gambling and drinking away the small money he makes from his vulcanizing business, but I will not allow him to rub cow shit on my face. To think that I gave up everything I would have become and followed that man. His dreams, if he had any, became mine. Your father beat me because I refused that he will bring one of those chicken peri-peri girls that serve food at Mama Tiro's restaurant into this house as his new wife. I swore by the mushrooms on my mother's grave never to allow it happen." Nwakaego's mother blinks and flicks off the cluster of tears clinging to her lower eyebrow. "Lagos is a long journey. Go and rest, Nwakaego."

Nwakaego slumps on the thin mattress at the foot of the loom, closes her eyes and begs for sleep to come.

Kpa. Kpa. The loom continues to work the edges of the *lappah*.

❋   ❋   ❋

As usual, her father is sprawled in the wooden lounger on the veranda. He hums and thumps his chest to the tune of a popular highlife beat that has *no woman, no wahala* in its chorus. It is well into the night now; the udala tree at the centre of the compound has swallowed half of the full moon.

"Good evening, Papa."

"I thought you will not come and greet me." The old man clasps his hands together and draws them to his sides.

Nwakaego forces out a smile. "It's not like that, o. I was sleeping. The bumpy journey rearranged my bones and I did not want to disturb when you were snuffing *utaba* with your friends."

"Your mother must have told you her side of the story."

"Emm ..."

"Nwakaego, you should understand that men have needs and at your mother's age, she cannot meet some of these needs. Do you know my blood has stopped rushing when your mother touches me in bed?" He grins and gives Nwakaego a playful nudge. Seeing that his daughter does not as much as budge, he stops grinning. "Why is your face like shovelled dung? Learn how to smile. It is this type of face that will chase men away from you. Your mother's renouncement is enough husband-repellent, don't make it worse." The old man springs up from the chair and goes into the house.

Nwakaego has always wanted to be the perfect daughter for her father, but there is always a hole in the wall echoing that she is never enough, that no matter how she stretches herself, he will not look at her with the same eyes he looks at his sons with. All these years, she has continued to skin herself for her father's approval – maintained an impeccable academic record, taken his side in his many squabbles with her mother, got into Harvard on full scholarship and nearly forfeited her passion for economics to study engineering. Maybe it is time she stopped.

*   *   *

Her mother is not in the room when she wakes

up. The door is unlocked, so Nwakaego knows her mother has gone to the stream to announce her renouncement to the world.

"Sister Nwakaego, good morning," the twins, Chima and Chime, chorus as she walks into the parlour.

"See my *ejima*, oo! They are now taller than me. When did you people come back?"

Chime, the taller of the twins, answers. "Around midnight. Brother Emeka picked us up at Lokoja."

"See as you dey shine. You dey chop Lagos money alone." Chima, the older one, tugs at Nwakaego's cheeks.

"Have you had breakfast?"

"Yes, Ifebuche fried *akara* and made *akamu*."

"Who is Ifebuche?"

"Our new wife. Sorry, Papa's new wife."

The twins have already started squashing the memories of their mother to make room for *our new wife* in their hearts, even before the renouncement is complete.

Outside the house, Emeka, their father and a woman are talking in low tones. The woman, who is just a tad older than Nwakaego, has her hands wound around Nwakaego's father's waist. She must be Ifebuche.

"Papa, good morning. Brother Emeka, good morning," Nwakaego mumbles a perfunctory greeting as she walks past them. They do not respond.

● ● ●

In the evening, the house begins to fill with people. The canopies beside the gate are crammed with the sweaty bodies of aunties, uncles, nephews, nieces and cousins. Nwakaego's father and other members of the Oriego Age Group are downing shots of schnapps in the parlour. They are patting his back and telling him to *dibe*, that he should endure, that his new wife will be a good replacement for *that heartless woman*.

Four women, wearing long, flowing gowns, drag Nwakaego's mother to the centre of the compound. One of the women, Ogoli, slaps Nwakaego's mother and spits at her. The other two, Ure and Ugo, rip her *lappah* into pieces. The crowd jeers and the naked woman cups her face in her palms.

"You are a failed woman, nobody will ever need you," Ogoli says as she grabs Nwakaego's mother's breasts. She places a hot rod over each nipple until she is satisfied they are sealed. Then she smears *nzu* on each of the burnt tips.

Nwakaego turns her face away. Chima and Chime have been holding her hands the whole time to stop her from disrupting the renouncement ritual.

The crowd disperses as the ceremony winds to an end. Nwakaego's mother is free now.

● ● ●

"Nwakaego, you have to listen to me. No man is ever worth giving up your dreams for," Nwakaego's mother says as she zips the last of her boxes. "Before your father married me, I wanted to be a –"

"Mama, look!" Nwakaego gasps. "Milk is dripping from your left breast!" She rummages through her handbag for a tissue paper to dab the wet patch on her mother's blouse.

"This is impossible." Nwakaego's mother removes her blouse. "You see these three veins on my left breast? They are for your father, Emeka and you. The vein pumping milk is yours."

"What does this mean?"

"That you still need me. Set me free, Nwakaego, let me go."

"I don't know how to set you free."

"Nwakaego, your breast is also dripping milk. Do you realize what this means? That I am now a burden to you, and you are also a burden to me. But I will keep this a secret. I don't want to ruin your life."

"Why keep it a secret?"

"You will be banished from your father's house if he gets to know about this. And I know how you are your father's daughter."

"Maybe I am not my father's daughter after all. Maybe I am my mother's daughter." Nwakaego holds her mother's hands. "Come with me to Lagos. You've always wanted to see the world; the world is in Lagos."

"Lagos or no Lagos, you are the world I want to see."

So the daughter kisses her mother's forehead and they wait, in this dimly lit room, for nightfall, when they will leave and no one can see them.

WHEREVER MISTER JENSEN WENT

REYAH MARTIN

Mister Jensen lives outside of town. He lives where the killins happen, the shootins an' all the most mysterious things. He's got a black face an' black eyes an' lips that's pink with too much flesh. He's hunchbacked an' angry an' mutters in some other tongue, an' on the right side of town they say his cane is made from human bones. *Bonesa kids maybe*, says old ladies. They scrunch they brows under black hats, bulgin' under they good Sunday dresses. *Gotta be careful now. 'Specially 'round people like him.* They ain't many people like Mister Jensen. Maybe that's why they gotta be so careful. Nobody ever said, but ever'body knows that he's far away for a reason. Ever'body knows it's meant to be this way.

He sits in the swingin'-seat on his porch, kickin' himself back an' forth, danglin' from the tree-branch smokin' his pipe. The kids cycle up the dusty road on they daddies' old bikes to whisper about him. He's always watchin' 'em, eyes slit-small in the smoke-screen, an' some say even the crickets are quiet for him. They don' sing in the evenings roun' his house, jus' set and click a couple times, an' hide in his yellow-grass yard. The flies are quiet too, buttin' heads at the screen-door. He's forever slappin' 'em off his face. Most times he kills 'em. They land at his feet, an' his great big dog sleeps on they bodies.

The kids watch him all day, an' at night they make up stories. *Mister Jensen don' smoke tobacco. Smokes fly-blood instead, an' dust from the wind. Mister Jensen ain't got nobody. Killed his wife an' all his kids. Keeps a gun behind the screen door. An' he ain't never prayed in his life. Man won't never get to Heaven.*

Least that's what the kids say. Then they hurry home an' have they supper, an' put they daddies' ol' bikes in the ol' bike shed, an' if ever they talk about Mister Jensen they gets slapped straight in they faces. They mamas look like they jus' bit inta sour fruit: *Table ain't no place for talkin' like that.* They scowl, cuttin' they pork an' shakin' they heads. *No place for talkin' illa somebody. You understan' me?*

Then they mamas, always angry, look to they daddies. They daddies always gotta agree with they mamas, otherwise it's dangerous. Otherwise plates clatter, an' they mamas get dark an' moody, an' ever'body shouts. They shout an' shout an' sometimes somebody cries. Most times it's the mamas. They set wailin': *Ain't you gonna do nothin'? Don't this matter to you?*

Then they daddies put down they knives an' forks. They push they plates away an' yell: *Christ, Louisa, they chil'ren. How they supposed to know what's right and wrong?*

They daddies do a lotta watchin', smokin' they cigarettes with heavy furrowed brows. Sometimes they ain't even payin' attention, but they know when Mama gets mad. An' when Mama gets mad, Daddy does the spankin', but he don' say nothin', 'cause when he was a boy he talked ill at the table too, an' his own daddy always slapped hard. Makes him shudder thinkin' 'bout it. And thinkin' 'bout the sleepin' dog; how it snaps off flies' wings in its lazy lopsided mouth, its tongue sloungin' over its lips in the dry wind. It kills them with a whip-crack-snap, an' people say *that dog's gonna kill a man one day.*

They mamas say the same, when they're undressin' for bed. They lie bare-naked an' say they prayers, an' in secret they hopin' it kills Mister Jensen. But they never let they chil'ren know. Chil'ren already know too much. Chil'ren should be learnin' important things like they books an' they Scripture an' they own prayers. That's what ever' mama thinks, when she prayin' naked under the sheets.

●　　●　　●

News is awhile comin' from outta town. It's in the Sunday papers, an' it reaches the grand houses three days late. Crosses the green lawns, skirts the sheds an' hosepipes. The kids bounce up on they knees behind white fences, hidin' they faces behind they hands, shoutin' to the mailmen. The mailmen jump, laugh with they mouths but not they eyes. Measure they steps to the mailboxes, kicking up dirt. The kids hold newspapers like banners. They fight over who gives Daddy the news. They fight over who drinks his last sippa coffee, lickin' slips of thick foam from they mouths. An' Mama cooks and Daddy reads an' the chil'ren squabble till he takes his bath in the upstairs room. He does his readin' in the Sunday bath, tells Mama ever'thin' worth tellin'. She lies with him as he dries, laid up like a slab'a meat in the heat through the window. She's waitin' on the stories, but he's awful quiet today. All the fathers are quiet today. They's a lotta readin' in Sunday papers. Too much readin'. Gives all the fathers a headache. They call they wives inta the bedroom an' promises they chil'ren coffee tomorrow if they jus' git out an' play.

The chil'ren go. Then, quieter than flies, they daddies spit an' stutter:

Mister Jensen's gone, Louisa.

Him an' that great big dog.

Says here he killed himself in the night.

They wives look sticky with guilt. They fold they hands an' sink they heads, an' the chil'ren know bad things is comin'. They's backed up against the thin wall, holdin' they hands up at they faces to stifle the sounda they breath. Couple of 'em gasp, usin' words they mamas don' like. They get so caught up in listenin', bodies scrunched together, but they don' understand so it makes for more stories. One an' two an' three at a time the kids sidle over to the ol' bike sheds. They fumble in the musky dark, nostrils burnt with the sweet-oil smell, the rust crawlin' up handlebars. Somewhere in ever' grand house, ever' mama is cryin'. Ever' daddy got a headache from readin' the Sunday papers. Ever' kid gone out to play. They's only the rasp of a dry, dusty wind. That an' the soft hissa tires zippin' on the dusty road.

The chil'ren grind they tire tracks inta ruts an' bumps. They hoot like birds, chatterin' through a tangle'a bike chains an' creakin' brakes. One of them says he seen a man hidin' 'round the backa Mister Jensen's house. He seen a man three days ago with a great big gun, an' he heard the dog yowlin' in the night. They say *you talkin' trash. You was in town three days ago, tryin' on suits with you mama.* And he knows they's right so he shuts his mouth. But somethin' like that gits kids talkin'. They whisper before they's even at his house. They's slowin' down, searchin' in the spindly trees for the ghost of his great big dog.

Bet he's low down in the bushes. Still huntin' the flies.

You see that? Somethin' movin' there, I swear. Looks like ... looks like a man.

Don' make a sound. He might spring out from someplace. Kill you stone dead.

They eyes are fit to bust, tearful-red 'round the rims. They look like they gonna cry, but brave kids don' do that. They swear on they lives. *Ain't nobody goin' kill me. Nobody. Understan'? I ain't afraida no ghost.*

They pickin' up speed as the road thins down. They stop at the yellow-grass yard, an' just beyond there's the house, the windows all boarded up. They ain't nothin' but the seat swingin' from the tree branch. The seat an' a sheriff leanin' forward, eyes fixed straight ahead. If they're careful they can sneak up an' see his face. They flatten themselves inta the dirt, crushin' clodsa earth in they hands. They've never seen the sheriff so close up. He's talkin' a lot, chin wobblin'. His face hangs to the left a bit. He's turned away from the screen door, but they's somebody else on the inside. They's a lotta words springin' from behind the screen door. And they's another man there smokin' a cigarette. The chil'ren hold they breath from the smell.

Man's gone, alright. No question. Looks like he did it himself.

He's like a spider: huge round head an' thin hands, an' pinchin' the cigarette 'tween two fingers. *Woulda been a struggle, what with the hunchback an' all. A helluva struggle. You gotta wonder what drove him to it. God-awful thing to do.*

The chil'ren sit up on they knees, tumblin' on toppa each other. The hot air thickens with squabblin' an' insults. The shadow-man smokes his hangin' cigarette, spittin' ash through his front teeth. He finishes one an' another, an' all the time the sheriff's talkin'.

Seems a terrible lonely place. Big yard, little house. An' that big dog the only one to see him go. Not another livin' soul. Pretty sad, ain't it? Don't it strike you sad, James?

The sheriff sounds like a mama. He keeps askin' questions that nobody answers. James is watchin' him, hard, through the doorway. He crushes three cigarettes under his heel. He's thinner than the sheriff, with one'a those cold faces. Straight jaw an' steel-sharp eyes, teeth like a rat caught in a corner. He flashes them in the sunset. The chil'ren are still holdin' they breath. They're waitin' for the moment the dog springs out, knocks him flyin' in a clouda black ash. They're waitin' for Mister Jensen with his bone-marrow cane. Any second now he'll take his seat on the tree-swing. He'll smoke his pipe an' stare straight ahead an' send the Sheriff screamin' home to his mama. The kids hush theyselves in the far corner. They skin's marked where they've laid too long on the ground. They whisper on they elbows:

Any second now. Jus' you wait …

Mister Jensen's hiding, he's waiting in the dark …

Ol' Mister Jensen an' his great big dog ...

They's a hard silence: expectation. But they's no sign'a Mister Jensen. Not a hobblin' footstep. Not a low, lazy growl from a great big dog. Jus' the clicka ol' boots an' one ancient key. An' still the sheriff is talkin' an' talkin'. Foldsa chin-skin suckin' in an' out. He passes the pile'a ol' bikes, rust sneakin' like a snake over the seats an' the pedals, but it don't bother him. The kids clamp they mouths when the men hurry down the dirt road. They stretch they bodies stiff an' low, where the lasta sunset falls. Already the crickets are beatin' in the distance. They're loud tonight at Mister Jensen's house; so loud that they *click-clack* cries cut inta the chil'ren's heads. A fly or two settles on they bodies, an' for a second nothin' moves. A couple kids half-sigh, lettin' out the breath they been holdin' too long. They sit an' wait for Mister Jensen, past dusk inta the dark. In they grand houses, night is the time for stories. The time for trouble at the table. For wakin' all shivery from a bad dream. But tonight nobody sleeps.

Somebody cries: *I wanna go home!* But they's

no light left to find the bikes with.

Somebody cusses an' turns over, all angles an' elbows: *Get the hell off, you crushin' me!*

A shock-horror gasp ripples through the grass. Nobody can tell if it's breath or the breeze. At last somebody breaks the silence: *Man says he's gone, you know. An' if he's gone, it's empty.*

It's the same boy who still goes with his mama inta town. Can't be trusted to go alone. If it wasn't night-time, nobody'd listen to him. But the dark makes the chil'ren anxious. They gather near him, white-faced an' wide-eyed.

If it's empty, you know, we could go inside.

Check for his ghost. His real ghost.

An' look behind the door ... where he kept his gun!

They run. They run an' sneak inside, quieter'n flies. Under a steady half-moon the chil'ren search the house, stickin' they tiny intimate hands inta ever' corner. Takes jus' a second to look behind the screen door. An' jus' a second more to look ever'where else. By sunrise they've fallen asleep, heads squashed inta each other's shoulders, all crushed inta the ol' tree swing-seat. When they wake they decide that Mister Jensen musta gone forever. An' they musta been right 'cause he never came back.

●   ●   ●

Nobody talks 'bout him anymore. Not the mamas or the daddies or the chil'ren. Thing is, they's always someone else they can make up stories about. They's always somebody else who's far away for a reason. Even without Mister Jensen, things are almost the same. They mamas pray for other people an' they daddies still read every scrappa the Sunday papers. They's still coffee in the bottom'a the Sunday cups, an' the men still smoke instead'a listenin' to they women. But people know that things were never meant to be this way. Course, nobody ever found the gun or the ghost, or even the shadow of the great big dog. Nobody – not even the fat sheriff – found anything like that.

Some say he hid his gun right before he died, an' it's someplace nobody'd ever think to look. Some say he let the dog loose in the trees, an' on stormy summer nights you can hear it snappin' at the flies. Some say he's buried in his own backyard, where he buried his wife an' his chil'ren. Other people say he was jus' an ol' man, sad an' lonely an' struck with the grief. But nobody wants ta believe that him bein' gone is they own fault. Mamas an' daddies an' chil'ren sit quiet inside'a town.

The chil'ren start to understand. They don't say nothin' 'bout what happened, unless somebody asks. An' when somebody asks, they say: *Mister Jensen always lived outside'a town.*

They parents put down they coffee. The women stop they cookin', holdin' they hands to they hearts. The chil'ren keep talkin': *He always lived far away. Far away for a reason.*

They take a forkfulla they supper, press they lips together, thinkin' hard. Nobody knows if this counts as talkin' ill at the table. They mamas don' tell them no more, an' they daddies got no need to spank.

After all, ever'body knows ... They stop, unsure'a theyselves. Then the chil'ren say the safest thing they can thinka:

He lived where the killins happened
an' the shootins
an' all the most mysterious things.

MAFOOTOO

BRIAN S. HEAP

The people at Number 24 are lovely. They're Jamaican. Which is not unusual in itself, given what's happened to immigration in this country since the War. But they are lovely. They have fitted in so well. On this road, at any rate. We did have our concerns at first. But they are very quiet. Well, you hear such stories. Look at what happened in Tottenham. But you hardly ever hear or see the Grandisons at all.

Evadne stands at the window looking out at the two conspiring women in their shapeless coats, each clutching identical oversize shopping bags. Oh, the aesthetic duplicity of lace curtains! Designed to grace these bland front windows, they largely serve to prevent people looking into your private space. On the other hand, they are equally useful as camouflage when you wish to look out unobserved. Evadne thinks about how her Maroon ancestors once donned the cacoon vine as camouflage to ambush the English Redcoats. "Mafootoo," her Uncle Wentworth called it. The net foliage of the curtains now serves a similar purpose.

Not that their coats are red. More a sickly beige colour. *They're out there talking about us.* She can tell by the way they keep looking sideways in the direction of her house. Chat too much. And when you and them buck up it's, "Good morning, Mrs Grandison, lovely morning." *Old hypocrite dem.*

The house is silent. Evadne likes to have the radio on as a rule, but she's dressed and all ready to go, though the taxi won't be here for another half-hour. The front room is chilly for September. Hubert would be furious. He always keeps the house at around the same daily mean temperature as Jamaica, even in summer. But she is the one who has to worry about paying the heating bills, and she really doesn't mind the cold. Maybe something to do with growing up in the mountains. She was descended from the

Africans who fled to the most remote parts of the interior after it became clear to the Spaniards that the British would now be the ones to preside over the island's continued exploitation. She used to complain bitterly about the heat when she first moved down from the hills into Kingston. The government office where she worked was not air-conditioned, just so-so ceiling fans careening wildly off kilter above the workers' heads with little effect beyond churning the daytime heat like molasses.

She first met Hubert when she was having lunch in Times Store on King Street one day. The restaurant was heaving with the midday crowd of shopgirls and office workers, and she was sitting at a table for two by herself; he asked, pardon, but did she mind if he took this seat. She didn't mind, even though she was slightly annoyed at having to share her space with this "bwoy". He introduced himself as Hubert Grandison, and soon they were meeting for lunch on a daily basis. Then he took her to Carib to see a movie. *Phaedra* it was, starring Melina Mercouri and Anthony Perkins. That must have been just after all the Independence excitement in '62. *"I don't care if the whole world burns down. I'd sacrifice anything to kiss you."* Evadne chanted Melina's lines like a mantra. Hubert didn't like the show. How could a woman dash away a man's man like Raf Vallone for a softie like Perkins? Damned Greek foolishness!

The romantic part of things was not so easy between them at first. Evadne liked sex. She was a country girl. She wasn't promiscuous or anything like it, but she was from the hills and simply took sex in her stride. She enjoyed it. Hubert liked the idea of it but, if she was honest, he was a bit of a prude. And like a lot of men, he was better at the chase than the delivery. She shocked Hubert when she finally suggested to him that they should fuck. Even the word stunned him for a minute. But she was not one for beating about the bush, and she even unnerved some of her own family with how forthright she could be. Hubert was non-Maroon, *obroni*, somebody from beyond the horizon, an outsider, which is why her Uncle Wentworth opposed the match from the outset. Evadne's father was more supportive, believing that Hubert would offer his daughter a better life away from Jamaica: the boy had made it very clear that he planned to move them both to England at the earliest opportunity.

The clock ticking. The smell of lemon furniture polish. The faded print of an African girl above the fireplace. Evadne's eyes wander around the tidy front room until they land on a small wooden bowl with the words PORT ANTONIO, JAMAICA, W. I. that somebody had burned into it with a hot metal spike.

I remember when we bought that, she thinks. *It was when we went back home for Daddy's funeral.* Uncle Wentworth still didn't like Hubert, but in deference to his niece, he put on his best face. Even liveried in the mafootoo withe over his best suit, his white shirt dazzling against his dark complexion, he was still diminished. Wentworth's loss of his only brother hung on him like that same cacoon vine, as though the little trailing bush around his shoulders were reaching to the earth below, to draw him into the ground to rejoin his lost sibling, his fellow warrior.

There had been a lot of drumming and singing; men and women, with agility belying their years, moved gracefully in honour of the deceased around the specially constructed booth woven from bamboo and coconut fronds. An abundance of overproof rum, along with coffee, hard dough bread, crisp fried sprats, jerked pork and curried goat were served at different intervals throughout the night – the wake had gone on till morning. Evadne, as chief mourner, had struggled to stay awake that afternoon during the extended funeral proceedings. It seemed as if everybody in the parish needed to get up and make a tribute to her father. It had been an exhausting week, what with the grave digging, nine nights and constant stream of visitors to deal with. That's why Hubert had taken her to the hotel in Port Antonio for a few days to recuperate. She wouldn't be coming back for the tombing. She would send some money, of course, but that was a ceremony that would have to take place without her.

Startled by the ringing of the doorbell, Evadne gets up from her place on the couch, peeps around the lace curtains and waves to the young Asian taxi driver standing by the porch. He's early. She puts on her coat quickly and picks up her handbag, checking that she has her taxi fares and door key. By the time she gets outside she realizes that the two beige coats and big shopping bags are still there, craning their necks to see whom she is leaving with. Evadne softly kisses her teeth before nodding almost imperceptibly in their general direction as she gets into the back seat of the waiting car.

"*As-salaamu alaykum*, Zafar," Evadne greets the young driver.

"*Wa alaykumu s-salaam*, Mrs Grandison." Zafar expresses no surprise at her use of the Islamic greeting. "Where to?"

Evadne gives him his directions, and clicks on her seat belt. The first time she heard the *salaam* in England, she had been startled by the greeting; she had often heard it used by her father, Uncle Wentworth and the members of the Maroon Council. Its familiarity immediately connected her to the Asians with whom she came into contact in the area of London where she and Hubert had first settled. One or two were quite surprised to hear the greeting from a Jamaican woman, who was not obviously of their faith. But now it was not unusual for Evadne even to send a "Happy Eid" card to the waiters at the local Bangladeshi restaurant at the end of the holy month of Ramadan. She had forgotten to ask Uncle Wentworth about the *salaam* when she went back for the funeral. Now she would probably never know where it came from among her own displaced people. Settling back into these and other thoughts, Evadne suddenly begins to feel a slight uneasiness about how this particular taxi journey is going to end.

When they had first come to England, Hubert travelled ahead by himself to sort out his work and their accommodation; then he sent for Evadne and their infant son, Basil. They had named the baby after Hubert's father, a police officer who was said to have died tragically in the line of duty when a fully laden truck rolled back and pinned him to a wall as he patrolled the market. At their wedding, Evadne discovered something Hubert either hadn't told her or didn't know himself: a drunken relative, lamenting that the older Basil wasn't there to see his one son get married, had told her: "You know, them say he died in the line of duty. But Basil had no business to be patrolling in the market that day. Is one young higgler gal from country he was checking when the truck mash him up." Nevertheless, when Hubert decided that he wanted to name his son for his long-dead father, Evadne went along with it and continued to keep that secret – along with many others – to herself.

*　　*　　*

There he lies in the hospital bed, hidden among his own camouflage, his mafootoo now a thicket of tubes and wires, the tendrils of some alien species. She hardly recognizes Hubert in the maze of coils and cables. The only sound emanating from this entanglement is the regular beep of the machine that monitors his life signs. Evadne suddenly remembers something she heard during a Sunday school lesson in Jamaica sixty years earlier. She can't be sure, but she thinks it might have been a version of the

Apostles' Creed:

> *He ascended into Heaven,*
> *And sitteth on the right hand of God, the Father*
> *Almighty,*
> *From thence He shall come to judge the quick*
> *and the dead.*

In her juvenile mind, Evadne had visions of hordes of her classmates making some slick manoeuvres, scattering in all directions out of harm's reach, so as not to be caught up with the dead in the Judgment thing. It was years later that her son had explained to her that "quick" meant "alive". ("Well, Basil, I wasn't that far off," she had said irritably.)

Now she looks at her husband of fifty years, trussed up like a bewildered Christmas tree, all trailing streamers and twinkling lights, undecided about whether he is quick or dead.

When she first got the phone call from the hospital and realized how serious it was, the rage that hit her took her by surprise. Look at how long he's been planning to retire. Why are we still here? Because of the house? The pension? The healthcare? Or because if we go back, some unconscionable scamp is going to rob us of everything we have spent our lives accumulating? Hubert's voice comes to her now as clear as the day it had been when he had called her out of the kitchen to read to her from *The Weekly Gleaner*.

"Evadne, you know what them bad man in Jamaica are saying now? That when they go out and kill people, they making duppy. Can you imagine, Vads? Making duppy! You never hear nuttn' so in all your life?"

Now she looks across at Hubert in the bed. "Is that what I am here to do? Make duppy? Is that what this is?"

Evadne's outlook on death is not unlike her approach to sex. Direct. Sometimes disconcertingly so to others. She studiously avoids the plethora of euphemisms adopted so enthusiastically by those around her:

"Evadne, what year was it that your dear father passed?"

"Passed what? Urine? His Common Entrance exam?"

Evadne is not a big churchgoer. In the early days, she and Hubert had gone for worship in the private homes of other Jamaicans, as much for social and moral support as spiritual. Later on, she began to find their company tedious. "I didn't come all this way here with you to create Jamaica all over again in foreign," she told her husband. Instead, choosing to struggle against a ferocious headwind, she worked her way through the bigotry, rejection and racism and did her own thing. How else was she to have a career, or ever to make her own way in this grey and alien place?

Her Maroon ancestors had been labelled traitors by some other Jamaicans for their treaties with the British, and for returning runaways to the very masters who enslaved them. But Evadne was having none of that. You needed to ally yourself with those who knew the ways to survive, who knew how to become invisible, how to merge with the landscape. So she went to an Anglican church. Blended into the mixed congregation. Detached. No pressure to join in any hearty fellowship. Evadne attended mainly for the hymns, which she enjoyed singing in her rich contralto voice noted more for its volume than for its tunefulness. It was a voice better designed for calling across wide valleys, or for bouncing off sheer mountain slopes. Nevertheless, she was enthusiastic, and was particularly fond of the Charles Wesley hymn "And Can It Be that I Should Gain?". She liked it because it was a hymn that posed questions, unlike so many others that made enormous assumptions about the depth of one's faith. *Amazing love, how can it be, that Thou my God, should'st die for me?* The imagery of chains falling off, with the accompanying release into freedom, held a particular resonance for her.

At this time in her life, many of Evadne's friends were now "transitioning" – another euphemism for death that she had actually grown to associate, thanks again to Basil Junior, with something called "gender reassignment". So she continued to alarm people with her unfiltered, disarmingly forthright condolences. "Sorry to hear your husband dead" to an already distraught widow, or: "The man all healthy and doing his daily jogging one minute, and next thing you know him is as dead as a nit." Not for her those lofty, evasive expressions like "moving to another phase of life" or "elevating to a higher plane" or "entering into glory" or even "returning to the Ancestors / Mother Earth".

"Him dead?" The question is directed to a slightly plump and freckled nurse with red hair, dressed in a navy blue tunic and matching trousers.

"Well, Mrs Grandison," replies the nurse after quickly composing herself and continuing in a lowered tone: "We're not seeing any significant brain activity." An Irish lilt, confirmed by her badge: NURSE PHELAN.

"It's the machine keeping him alive, nuh?"

"Indeed, yes, Mrs Grandison. Mr Grandison is on what we call a respirator."

"I know what it is. Plug him out."

"I beg your pardon, Mrs –"

"Me say, plug him out."

"But, Mrs Grandison, I'm not authorized to do that."

"So find me somebody who is. I am the next

of kin." (...*Who shall come to judge the quick and the dead* steals into her head as an afterthought.)

At first Nurse Phelan is uncertain what to do next, but responds to Evadne's commanding stare and the fierce set of her jaw by disappearing through the door in search of reinforcements.

Evadne moves slowly towards the bed, searching for something of Hubert and his personality that she can address directly. Eventually, she begins to softly intone his name.

"Hubert, Hubert, Hubert. How you could do me like this? No warning? Nothing? Look how me stick by you all these years. Letting you follow your ambitions even when they never seemed like a good idea to me. Working your long, long hours. For what? More stress? Well, you get the stroke that you worked for. Four holidays in fifty years, not counting Daddy's funeral. A week in Cornwall when Basil got into grammar school. A long weekend for the two of us in Stratford-upon-Avon. A few days in the Lake District after Basil did his Duke of Edinburgh Award. And an overnight stay in Brighton one bank holiday.

"You never even went back for your own

mother. Left it to your sister to bury her. Look how me and you nearly parted when Basil brought his first boyfriend home. You were like a baby. Taking to your bed for the best part of a month. Couldn't deal with your shame. There were times when I really didn't like you. But I did know that in your own mind, you were seeing yourself as somebody honourable. A good provider. A successful businessman. Upstanding citizen. More British than the British.

"But you were selfish, Hubert, always limiting yourself to what was most familiar to you. Sending parcels back to Jamaica for community projects, but never dealing with the real issues. I have tried with this country, Hubert. I've tried with you. Basil will make his own happiness, with whoever makes him happy. But right now I don't know what to do. I feel like I stayed too long. I don't feel like I belong here. And I don't belong anywhere else.

"I never told you this, but when we first came here, even though we were struggling, I would save a little back each month and go to the post office and buy a postal order to send to your mother. Even though things were not great for us, I just felt that she had to eat a food too. And do you know what happened, Hubert? One day, before she died, a brown envelope came from Jamaica with some papers in it for me to sign for a land title issued in my name. She had taken all those trifling postal orders and saved them up and bought a small piece of land in the hills above Kingston, and got somebody to build a neat little cottage on it. One of your nephews lives there with his girlfriend, but they know it's mine. Basil took his friend there one time. But we had to keep it a secret, we couldn't let you find out. You weren't ready for that.

"So, Hubert, I think what I'm going to do is go and have a nice long holiday there by myself. And maybe then I will be able to decide where it is that I really belong. Or I will just straddle the Atlantic and simply come and go whenever I feel like it."

●   ●   ●

"Excuse me, Mrs Grandison. This is Dr Patel."

"*As-salaamu alaykum*, Doctor," a distracted

Evadne replies.

Dr Patel, born into a Hindu family in Glasgow, replies with a polite: "Yes, quite."

The process of switching off the life support machine proves to be rather more taxing than Evadne has envisaged. It involves having to be counselled by the care team; visits from a number of people in the hospital administration; the need to prove kinship; signing numerous forms; and calling on the services of a medical technologist. When the deed is finally done, Evadne waits for the machine monitoring Hubert's vital signs either to stop beeping altogether or to flatline into a continuous high-pitched whine, just like she has seen on television or at the pictures.

Only it doesn't.

Like a spite, Hubert keeps on breathing on his own.

The care team, Nurse Phelan, Dr Patel and a technologist appear to be almost embarrassed by this unexpected turn of events. Evadne just looks stunned. Slowly, the team members begin to drift away, leaving Nurse Phelan to bring a chair for Evadne to sit on and keep vigil. Eventually,

Evadne sits alone, listening to the monotonous beeping. She is in unknown territory now.

"Stop your fooling, Hubert," she whispers. "Just be quick and dead."

THE ART OF WAVING

ANDREA E. MACLEOD

I was seven when my sister taught me you did not have to wave at people just because they waved at you. I asked her if she meant like when we were standing in the bank line with our dead mother's boyfriend. It was just after she had died, and the guard sitting at the door winked and waved. My sister said waving was social influence and "if we are not careful other people will make us what we are". She also said: *I expect nothing from you. You are neither a flower nor a thorn*. When she turned seventeen, she got a tattoo with words that might have been by a Sufi poet. It said BE MELTING SNOW. She said it meant "let everything and everyone wash away from you". I said that made me sad, and she told me to grow up. She said *it's not sad, it's powerful*. She mouthed the word a second time, slowly, so later it felt like it had settled as a layer of my own skin.

As I grew older she insisted I understand why it was that in the Yale psychologist Stanley Milgram's 1961 experiment, 65 per cent of people administered electric shocks of the highest level to their fellow volunteers – even though they had been told that increasing the voltage could hurt or seriously injure the participant. I told my sister I would never do that, but she only raised her eyebrows and said people have a way of doing as they are told. Then she took my hand to show me all the children walking in a line, holding hands on their way into the school.

Now that I am twenty-seven I choose to wave to the woman who walks her black poodle every day at 7 AM, and puts blue gumboots decorated with pictures of tiny bones on his paws when it is raining. When it is hot he has yellow sneakers with polka dots; sometimes the poodle wears a bowtie. He is not wearing one today but it is Sunday; it is a day of rest. I do not wave to the woman who lives next door to us with her Cartier watch and Gucci sunglasses. Not because of those things, because if I had the money I would probably buy them, too. I do it because of how the woman walks past people in a way that reminds me of what people do when foul air strikes their nostrils. I also do not wave to the homeless man with the black cart living on the bench near the entrance to the supermarket. This homeless man waves to people, he waves to them as if he knows them *hi, hi, it's been so long, hi* and then, if they fall for his trick of familiarity, he will ask them for money. If you do go to this homeless man, who smokes skinny cigarettes with his thick sausage fingers and smells like lamb's fat and you do not give him money, he will spit on you. Some days the homeless man is like the snake that bit our mother when she was a child but had no venom because before it had bitten her, it hit the horse and the goat. This homeless man, when he's all dried up, makes this ghastly phlegmatic sound, which is almost worse than the spit, and the sound rattles in your head long after. It can become the beat of your dreams if you let it. Sometimes I think I would give him the money if he didn't spit on me. My sister tells me to spit back on him.

I was only nine when I took to practising the art of not waving without my sister around. I stonewalled my fifth-grade teacher when she waved as I crossed outside her classroom. I felt an exhilarating power surge inside me and I ran all the way home, punching the air as I went. I honed the art of disaffection when the local priest waved to invite me to join the Easter egg hunt. I told my sister and she was proud, patted me on the head the way our mother had and kissed my forehead. She said: "It's your choice, Mjolnir," and laughed. She said Mjolnir could level mountains, and I could too. She gave me lots of names. "Palu", for the intoxicating ironwood tree she read about once – *little fire berry*. But my favourite was something our mother used to say: *little dove*. To that my sister added: *rising out of the nigredo*.

When I was eleven I started to obsess about why we waved at all. Where did it come from? Why one hand and not two? I had no idea when I was eleven that some people waved with both hands. I did not reach that level of enthusiasm for years. One observer, on a late night Internet search, on an obscure website that may or may not have been written by a legitimate anthropologist, wrote that it was possible the first men pasted their handprints on cave walls to greet future visitors. The article was titled "A Wave from the Past". Then there were the studies on hand gestures, none of which could accurately detect when people began to wave – only saying that Queen Elizabeth II had one of the most famous waves, and that waving was once a popular activity in farewelling, seafaring folk, passengers on trains and loved ones heading to war.

I haven't decided whether or not to wave at the new FedEx man – who might be Iranian, because my sister, who overheard someone speaking with him, says his name is Dalir, which means *brave* in Persian. I think if I was Iranian I would want my name to be "Yesfir", which means *star* – together we would make *brave star*. But I am not Iranian. I know nothing much about Iran except where it is located, and that the longest river is called the Karun. Our mother told us, once, "the river is everywhere". It is from a book she loved, called *Siddhartha*.

Dalir has skin that is the shade of weak coffee and eyes that remind me of the hues in magnolia leaves that have been spent from the tree for more than a week. My skin is the colour of curdled milk, and if I spend a week in the pool over summer my hair still turns green even though someone told me I should have grown out of this by now because how many green-haired blonde women do you see, except for those who have used a home tint and resemble the variegated pineapple mint plants that have run amok in our tiny garden.

Dalir began our mail route six weeks ago, which I know because my sister noticed on Facebook that Evan, the guy who'd had the run before, had been hit walking home after work and was still in the hospital. My sister says Dalir might be the cousin of the Iranian man two blocks down from us, because she watched Dalir go inside the apartment and he still didn't come out after three hours, which was when she had to leave. The Iranian man, who sometimes tunes pianos but often is unavailable to work, doesn't wave at anyone either. He makes me wonder about why he stopped waving.

I know an Iranian woman called Anoosheh who is my age and works as a receptionist at the local dentist's. Sometimes she waves when I walk past the dentist's surgery and I wave back. We had some classes together in school, which is why I wave. I remember in English sometimes the teacher would ask her to write stories about what it was like in Iran, but instead she wrote about how a goat her cousin owned followed her to school. Someone asked did the goat get killed in the war. Anoosheh said no, the goat is not dead. It lives with my uncle. We told Anoosheh she could talk to us about her experiences in Iran because *we understood*, which was what the teacher told us to say. When new refugees arrived on the small, clapped-out refugee crisis centre bus and drove right past a group of us standing at the bus stop, everyone except me waved. Everyone on the bus waved to us, except Anoosheh. Anoosheh is the only person other than my sister that I have met who understood.

Everyone expected Anoosheh to have shrapnel scars or burns somewhere on her body from when the bombs fell on her house, because this is what we imagined happened to her. They thought she probably wanted to tell them the story about the Iranian scientist who left his wife and daughter at home and, riding to work on his motorbike, was blown up, perhaps because someone thought he was a supervisor at the plant where scientists were suspected of working on a nuclear weapon. Or how towards the end of the Iran – Iraq War in 1988, a US Navy ship called the *USS Vincennes* shot down Iran Air Flight 655, killing all civilian passengers onboard.

But Anoosheh didn't want to talk about any of that. She didn't say much at all. One day when she got undressed in the showers, some of the girls climbed the cubicle to get a better look, but she didn't have any scars that they could see. I still think everyone was amazed when finally she told us this ordinary story about how nobody stops for anyone crossing the road in Iran, meaning so many people die every year just stepping out onto the street. It was probably a year after she told us that story that we learned this was how her mother had died. Anoosheh had been holding her mother's hand when a truck hit them. I learned this because someone told someone, who passed it on until I was told. When a local boy was killed recently at a crossing on a WALK sign, Anoosheh (which means *fortunate*) was quiet for a week. She did not wave to anyone. I tell my sister, you know that girl Anoosheh who works for the dentist. My sister says yes, and then, disapprovingly, the one that you wave at. I say yes. I think she was lying about the goat.

My sister follows Dalir from the mail depot. He rides a bike that was given to him by the refugee crisis centre. This is obvious, because the paint is scratched up and it has two different tires on it and nobody has anything second-hand these days unless they get it from the crisis centre. My sister hears that just after Dalir got the bike someone hung a sign on it that said DALIR FUCKS CAMELS, and the bogan guys from the housing commission still wrap towels around their heads and throw rocks at Dalir when he rides past. I wish a river would rise up and engulf them.

My sister says Dalir's unit at the centre is in the same block where three girls were raped last year at a party. I remember there were no charges laid. In the paper, the photo of the girls showed them laughing and holding firecrackers to the sky. When one of them hanged herself six months later and word got out that she was pregnant, people got angry on social media but now nobody remembers the dead girl's name. It might have been "Dewar", which I read somewhere means *stranger*, but it might also mean *beautiful*.

I decide to steal a letter from the Iranian man to find out his name. I find a handwritten envelope with small neat handwriting that says MR F. SHAHROUDI. That night I look up his name on the Internet. I find just one entry that could match. It is for a "Farhad Shahroudi". The Internet tells me a Mr Farhoud Shahroudi was a member of the Iranian National Orchestra, and disappeared in 1996. He has one daughter. When I look up "Iran events 1996", I find a transcript of an interview with a Tehran police chief that outlines that the testimony of a man who claimed he was beaten and held captive by Iranian forces was not credible, even though the man was later given asylum to live in the United States. I also read that the police chief was paid a large sum of money to say these things, but that this fact might also not be true. In *The New York Times* there was a story about an Iranian man who was beaten and lost six teeth from malnutrition in a Tehran prison. The man had one daughter. I take a screenshot of Mr Farhad Shahroudi. Later, when I see the Iranian man from two blocks down, F. Shahroudi, taking out the trash, I take a photo of him. A real photo that I can hold to the light and trace his figure with my eyes. I feel certain it is the same man. I begin to wonder how I can know if he is Mr Farhad Shahroudi the famous Iranian pianist, or Mr Farhad Shahroudi who lost his wife when her plane was shot down and has six false teeth.

Yesterday my sister found a book of poetry in our letterbox by Forough Farrokhzad. It has a page turned down at the poem called "The Wave". It has my name written in pencil above the title. It begins: *To me you are a wave; never here, never there! You are – still – nowhere!* In that moment, I see the Wave and my mother's river everywhere. And I see that even if I wave to Dalir, it does not mean that he will wave back.

AUTHOR BIOGRAPHIES

Kritika Pandey
(Overall winner and regional winner: Asia)
Kritika Pandey is a Pushcart-nominated Indian writer and a final-year MFA candidate at the University of Massachusetts, Amherst. She is a recipient of a 2020 grant from the Elizabeth George Foundation. Her works are forthcoming or have appeared in a number of literary magazines in the US, India and elsewhere. She has won the Harvey Swados Fiction Prize, the Cara Parravani Memorial Award and the Charles Wallace Scholarship for Creative Writing at the University of Edinburgh.

Innocent Chizaram Ilo
(Regional winner: Africa)
Innocent Chizaram Ilo is an Igbo writer from Nigeria. Their works interrogate gender, class, memory and sexuality, and have been published

in literary magazines across four continents. They are a finalist of the Gerald Kraak Award, Short Day Africa and Wilbur Smith Author of Tomorrow prizes, and have also won the Africa YMCA and Oxford Festival of the Arts short story contests. Their works have been published widely in international anthologies and periodicals.

Reyah Martin
(Regional winner: Canada and Europe)

Born in Scotland, Reyah Martin has featured in several online publications and was a finalist in the BBC Young Writers' Award 2018. She is a member of the Scottish National Youth Arts Advisory Group, and an undergraduate of Journalism and Creative Writing at Strathclyde University. When she is not writing, she tutors English and Creative Writing with a focus on encouraging young people. She is currently working on her debut novel.

Brian S. Heap
(Regional winner: Caribbean)

Brian S. Heap is retired Senior Lecturer, Staff

Tutor in Drama and Head of the Philip Sherlock Centre for the Creative Arts at the University of the West Indies, Mona, Jamaica. He has worked in Drama and Education in Jamaica for over forty years. He has co-authored two books on process drama (with Pamela Bowell), as well as several conference papers and articles for refereed journals. He served as Conference Director and Convener of the Fifth International Drama in Education Research Institute (2006) in Kingston, Jamaica. He was honoured with the Silver Musgrave Medal by the Institute of Jamaica in 2002.

Andrea E. Macleod
(Regional winner: Pacific)
Andrea E Macleod is a Brisbane writer, poet and journalist. In her journalism, she is passionate about issues of equality and justice. She is studying literature and working on a collection of short stories as well as a novella. Her work was shortlisted for the Newcastle Short Story Award and long-listed for the ABR Elizabeth Jolley Short Story Prize.

Selected Titles from Paper + Ink

Visit **www.paperand.ink** to subscribe and receive the other books
by post, as well as to keep up to date about new volumes in the series.